eter Potato

D0407714

Polly
Pomegranate

Radish

Tim Tomato

# The Garden Gang
# stories and pictures by

# Jayne Fisher

Twelve year old **Jayne Fisher** is the youngest ever Ladybird author. She was only nine years old when she wrote these charming stories about fruit and vegetable characters.

Writing and drawing aren't Jayne's only interests. She has studied for the ribbon awards of the Royal School of Church Music, and plays the classical guitar and the recorder. Jayne sews, bakes, reads avidly, plays chess and keeps two gerbils and breeds stick insects.

But it is perhaps her own little garden at home which gave her the ideas for these stories. Jayne's bold, colourful felt-tipped pen illustrations are bound to appeal to young children and we can all learn a few lessons from the characters in the 'Garden Gang'.

# Penelope Strawberry

Ladybird Books Loughborough

Miss Penelope Strawberry
was beautiful.
Miss Penelope Strawberry
was extremely beautiful.
In fact,
you might say she was
the most beautiful Strawberry
in the whole wide world.
She had big blue eyes
and golden hair.

But one thing
spoiled her beauty.
She was snooty
and vain,
and if anyone
said, "Hello", to her
she would just
stick her nose
up in the air
and glide away.

She wanted everyone
to admire her
but I'm afraid
she had no friends.

So she decided to move
to a new house
in the country.
It was a pretty little cottage
with a fine garden.
There was a pool
with a fountain
and some goldfish.

One day Miss Penelope
was sunbathing
on the lawn. Bees were
humming busily
and bright butterflies
flitted to and fro
amongst the tall flowers.
Suddenly a
large violet beetle made
a startling appearance
between two
Dandelion stalks.
"Hello," he said
in a deep voice,
as he looked shyly
at her dazzling beauty.
"Who are you?"

13

"Go away," she said rudely.
"Go away."
And she looked
at him spitefully
through her large
dark sunglasses.
"Deary me," said the beetle,
"you are certainly not
as nice as you look.
If this is how
you treat visitors,
it's a wonder you have
any friends at all."
And he promptly
disappeared
the way he had come.

As Penelope lay
sunning herself
she began
to think that perhaps
she had been
rather rude to people,
and this could be
the reason why
she had no friends.
She decided
there and then,
to hold a garden-party
and to invite everyone
in the village.
She made a list
of everything she needed . . .

17

Chocolate cake

Icecream

Jelly

Iced cherry buns

Sandwiches

Blancmange

Chocolate fingers . . .

and hundreds of
sausage rolls.

She quickly
went indoors
to write invitations
to everyone.
She asked
a friendly squirrel
to deliver them
that afternoon.

There was great excitement
on Blackberry Common
when people
opened their invitations
to Penelope's party.
They hurriedly got out
their best clothes
and polished shoes.
Miss Ladybird
put on her new dress
with seven spots.
Sebastian Squirrel
brushed his tail
till it shone.
And Miss Penelope
went to her hairdresser
to have a new hair-do.

When Saturday came,
the sun shone and
Miss Penelope's garden
was full of
happy, chattering people.
What a wonderful feast
they all had!
"Penelope Strawberry,"
they said, "is not only
the most beautiful
Strawberry in the
whole wide world,
but also the kindest."
After that she always
had the one thing
she had ever really
wanted . . .

# Friends!

# Roger Radish

Roger Radish was shy.
He lived in a
neat little cottage
at the corner
of the garden.
Although he was
brought up
in a large family
he was awfully,
awfully, awfully shy.

Whenever he saw
anyone coming,
he would either
run indoors
or hide behind
the nearest tree
or wall
and wait
until they had gone.

One morning
Roger Radish
was going for a walk
down the lane when
a friendly wizard
came up to him.
"Hello,"
said the wizard,
in a friendly way.
"Help!"
yelled Roger Radish,
and promptly
disappeared behind
a nearby
tree stump.

"Goodness gracious!"
said the wizard
to himself.
"What a performance!
I must really
try to do something
to help this poor Radish."
But before he could say,
"Wet wellies,"
Roger Radish
was just a speck
in the distance.

Now there is something
I forgot to tell you
about Roger Radish.
He was a very good swimmer
but nobody knew about this
except the wizard,
who had often watched
Roger secretly,
from the river bank.

37

"I have a plan,"
thought the wizard.
"I know how
I can help Roger Radish,
but I will have to wait
for the right moment."

A few days later
Roger Radish was
having a quiet walk
along the river bank.
The birds were singing
in the tall trees
and the sun
was hot on his back.
He was whistling
a little tune
and he felt
very happy.

Suddenly the wizard,
who was hiding
in the bushes,
knew that
the time had come
to work his spell.
He waved his wand
and a canoe came swiftly
down the river,
out of control.
In it were two
frightened little chives
screaming for help.

43

Without hesitating
or waiting,
Roger Radish plunged
into the deep water
and began
swimming strongly
to the sinking chives.
Soon he had
caught each one
by the arm
and was swimming
quickly back to
the river bank.

Little did he know
that a large crowd
had collected
on the river bank,
waiting for the hero
to return.
The wizard had
magicked them there,
of course.

47

How they all
clapped and cheered,
as a bedraggled
Roger Radish
pulled himself,
and the two little chives,
out of the river.
They gave him
big bunches of flowers
and said he was
very brave.
Everyone thought
he'd run away and hide,
but he just stood
and smiled happily
at everyone.
The wizard's plan
had worked.

49

Roger
Radish
was
no
longer
shy!

Colin Cucumber

Penelope
Strawberry

Oliver Onion

Percival Pea